Sue Johnston, has written for comics in the past. She had a husband, has 2 children and now 4 grandchildren. First book *GRAN Tour of the UK* had 2 passengers, Furry toys called; Dartmouth and Cuthbert. They did 2,600 miles round the U.K. having adventures en-route.

She has two important advisers who guide her stories, called Izzy and Lauren, who have been with her since the start when they were aged 4 and 5.

To Sue and Ralph, who urged the writer to buy Dartmouth, over 40 years' ago.

To Helen and David, who gave me Cuthbert, as my mascot on my GRAN Tour of the U.K.

In memory of my late husband Ray, who would be pleased at how busy I am!

To thank my two technological gurus who helped me go forth in this IT age.

Sue Johnston

DARTMOUTH AND CUTHBERT'S CAR ADVENTURES

AUSTIN MACAULEY PUBLISHERS™

LONDON • CAMBRIDGE • NEW YORK • SHARJAH

A CIP catalogue record for this title is available from the British Library.

ISBN 9781398401570 (Paperback)
ISBN 9781398401587 (ePub e-book)

www.austinmacauley.com

First Published 2022
Austin Macauley Publishers Ltd®
1 Canada Square
Canary Wharf
London
E14 5AA

To Austin Macauley Publishers, for their editorial advice.

To my main advisers Izzy and Lauren, who put me on the right track.

To my iPad, for good photos for each story and for my general text in "Pages".

Table of Contents

Synopsis

Dartmouth is a brown teddy bear who is very hairy, has big paws and tiny eyes. He is rather grumpy and knows a lot. He is always telling facts to Cuthbert. He has a very deep voice. He is about seven years old and known to Cuthbert, as Fishhooks.

His friend is Cuthbert, a small, young and green dragon. Cuthbert has a high squeaky voice, a very wiggly tail that flaps around everywhere and a tiny warm breath that hasn't started heating up yet. He is nearly five years old and known to Dartmouth as Squeezums.

Cuthbert has a very important Secret Cap that is magical. It is orange and yellow and very small. It has a ribbon loop ` goes off to London each day by train. Their twin boys, Oliver and Lewis, aged five are not allowed to sit in the front that is why the car toys are there.

"They argue too much about whose turn it is, and besides I don't always know which one is which from the side view," Mum explains.

The car toys are always up to mischief when the car is empty. On return of the family, no one knows how mysterious things have happened while they've been away.

But we do, don't we!

The adventures are aimed at four-to-six-year-old boys and girls.

The stories are written to read out loud; Dartmouth has a very deep voice and Cuthbert has a high, squeaky voice.

I like to leave room on each page of story for you to draw the car toys.

Introduction

Dartmouth and Cuthbert are two cuddly toys that enjoy long journeys in the family car.

Olly and Lewis are five-year-old twins. Dad goes to London every day on the train to work. Mum has the car. The twins can't sit in the front passenger seat as they argue whose turn it is so Dartmouth and Cuthbert cuddle together inside the front seat belt and get up to a lot of mischief together.

They both have nicknames; Dartmouth is 'Fishhooks' and Cuthbert is 'Squeezums'.

Cuthbert has a Secret Cap that is magical.

Dartmouth is a large hairy brown teddy bear; he has a deep voice and is very grumpy most of the time. Cuthbert is a small, green, young dragon with a squeaky high voice, he comes from Loch Ness. Luckily, his fire-breathing hasn't started yet so his breath is just warm. His tail is getting longer every day and sometimes he doesn't know what to do with it.

Part 1

Chapter 1

Snow

Mum has difficulty driving the car in the snow to take Olly and Lewis to school. Afterwards she manages to park near the shops.

"Let's open the window," whispers Cuthbert. He swishes his tail, rubs his Secret Cap and suddenly they are both covered in snow.

"Atishoo," calls Dartmouth as large flakes fly into the car.

"This is fun," says Cuthbert, waving his tiny tail in the air. Soon they are both looking like snowmen sitting on the passenger seat.

"Snow is made of ice crystals y'know, Squeezums, they can be used for making snowmen and igloos. They can blow into blizzards and also avalanches in the alps," says Dartmouth. Mum comes hurrying back with her arms full of shopping. Putting it all in the boot, she opens her door.

"Oh, dear, how did that window get open?" She reaches across and presses the button to shut it.

"Now I'll have to take you in and dry you before I pick up the boys," Mum says.

"This is lovely, by the fire. I'm dry now but my fur is messy," grumbles Dartmouth.

"Here's a joke coming, Fishhooks," says Cuthbert. "How do snails keep their shells shiny? They use snail varnish."

"Humph," says Dartmouth. Once they are all home after school, Cuthbert rubs the Secret Cap and they both jump down into the snow in their garden.

They have great fun trying to make a snowman. They work quickly then whizz back into the car before the boys come out. "Mum, look at our snowman," calls Olly.

"What is that other funny one at the side of yours?" asks Mum.

"Oh, we didn't notice that."

We know who made it, don't we!

Chapter 2
The Park

"I've got a picnic, boys; we'll go to the park," says Mum after school one day. They all jump out of the car, leaving Dartmouth and Cuthbert as usual on the front passenger seat.

"Let's go too, Fishhooks," calls Cuthbert. (Fishhooks is his nick name for Dartmouth.) He rubs his orange and yellow Secret Cap. It lets the car toys fly out of the car. Dartmouth and Cuthbert land on the grass.

Dartmouth stomps along slowly. Cuthbert skips and twirls around in the sunshine. Soon they both sit down. "Here's a joke coming, Fishhooks," says Cuthbert. "What is black and white and goes around and around? Answer: a penguin in a tumble drier!"

Maisie comes along; she is five. "I'll make you a daisy-chain necklace if you like." Her mum has just shown her how. Dartmouth and Cuthbert sit still as statues, neither of them move when there are humans around. Dartmouth feels ticklish with daisies around his neck. Maisie begins one for Cuthbert, but her mum calls her away before it is finished.

Dartmouth says, "Daisies grow in our lawn. They open at dawn; ours are white with yellow middles. They have thick stems that are excellent for making daisy chains, Squeezums."

Dartmouth and Cuthbert whisk back to the car. Oh dear, they've left the Secret Cap on the grass. Mum and the boys load all their things in the boot. "What have the toys got on?" asks Mum. "And where is Cuthbert's Cap?" Olly and Lewis climb out to look for it.

"Found it," calls Olly. Maisie has gone home, so no one can explain about the daisies. We can though, can't we!

Chapter 3

Rainy Day

"Oh dear we'll be late for school if you can't find your wellies boys." Mum is always having to hurry Oliver and Lewis to get in the car after breakfast. They have to sit in the back while Dartmouth and Cuthbert occupy the front passenger seat with the seat belt firmly around them. The boys would argue if they had to choose who sits in the front.

Oliver and Lewis both look identical, so even Mum and Dad can't always tell, at a glance, which is which twin.

The supermarket car park has some deep puddles after the rainstorm. "Rain comes from water vapour stored in black clouds in the sky y'know, Squeezums," says Dartmouth.

"Let's go and paddle, Fishhooks," says Cuthbert rubbing his Secret Cap. They fly out of the car.

Cuthbert swishes his tiny tail in the water. Dartmouth stands grumpily at the edge of the puddle getting splashes all over his fur. Suddenly, he finds a small bouncy ball on the ground. Back in the car, Cuthbert throws the ball everywhere. It lands on the floor at their feet. "Here comes a joke, Fishhooks," calls Cuthbert. "What is orange and sounds like a parrot? Do you know?"

"It's a carrot." Dartmouth says, "Humph." He never understands jokes.

"Where did that bouncy ball come from? Why is the car toys' fur all wet?" Mum always asks the questions when she gets in the car and the twins don't know the answers.

We do though, don't we!

Chapter 4

To the Seaside

"Auntie Jean is coming too to the seaside," say the boys together. Dartmouth and Cuthbert get a surprise. They have to sit on the back seat between Oliver and Lewis. Luckily, Cuthbert is wearing his Secret Cap. All the way there the car toys are being buffeted with the twins' elbows. At last everyone gets out, taking their chairs, picnic, sun umbrella and swimming things to the beach.

"Thank goodness," grumbles Dartmouth. Suddenly they are on the sand too. Cuthbert has rubbed the cap. The two furry chaps walk along the beach in the sunshine. They make very funny footmarks in the sand: big claw paws from Dartmouth, tiny dot ones for Cuthbert and a long curvy line in between. "There are over 400,000 grains of sand in a pawful, Squeezums," says Dartmouth, looking over his shoulder as they walk along the beach.

"Do you know what that is?" points Dartmouth looking behind him?

"It's my tail, Fishhooks," calls Cuthbert, skipping along making more fuzzy marks on the beach. "Let's paddle." He runs to the edge of the sea. "Oops the waves are chasing me."

Dartmouth looks down at his salty paws. Cuthbert gets wet up to his armpits. "This is lovely," he shouts.

Ding, ding, ding – the Secret Cap is warning them to go back to the car. They make the middle of the back seat very damp. "Here's my joke, Fishhooks," calls Cuthbert. "How do all the seas say hello to each other?"

"Humph," says Dartmouth.

"They wave, ha-ha," says Cuthbert.

"Boys, you didn't dry yourselves very well," says Mum when they get home and empty the car. Auntie Jean waves bye as she walks home.

Now I must get the hairdryer out for that middle seat at the back, thinks Mum putting the car toys back in their usual place. I don't know how it got so wet.

We know though, don't we.

Part 2

Chapter 5
Mordington Scottish Borders

"Squeezums! Lovely long sticks." The twins have left their sticks from the woods in the front of the car. "Let's take them." The Secret Cap flies the car toys out onto the lovely Clappers grassy green lawn in the village.

"Boohoo. Mine's too long on this grass," grumbles Dartmouth plodding around holding his long stick.

"Follow me, Squeezums!" Cuthbert runs around and around the Clappers sign waving his stick in the air.

"I'm dizzy now. Let's plant them like Mum does in the garden at home Fishhooks."

They both push hard. Each stick is left in the middle of Clappers Green. "Wood grows as trees and branches Squeezums," says Dartmouth, preparing to give Cuthbert some facts. "Some names of trees are: oak, beech, silver birch, chestnut. We get conkers from horse chestnut trees y'know in autumn," Dartmouth says. "Are you listening Squeezums?"

The Secret Cap is whistling so they fly back into the car.

"How did our sticks get here?" calls Oliver as he rescues them from the green. We know, don't we!

Auntie Alice lives at the Old School House nearby which has an enormous library. She has invited the family in for tea.

"Bring the car toys, they can sit on the sofa," says Auntie, "we'll have our cream tea in the dining room."

"We're inside, Squeezums," says Cuthbert.

"Here comes my joke, Fishhooks, what is orange and sounds like a parrot? The answer is: a carrot!"

"Humph," says Dartmouth.

"I see a lovely book about giraffes." As Cuthbert pulls it off the library shelf, ten more books crash to the table, knocking over a vase of flowers. Rubbing his Secret Cap,

Cuthbert flies to sit back on Dartmouth's lap. Oliver and Lewis come in.

Mum arrives. "What are you up to, twins? What a mess I have to clear up now. How did that happen?"

We know, don't we.

Chapter 6
Soggy Fizz

Someone has put a bottle of fizz in the glove pocket of the dashboard with a loose lid. Suddenly, it sprays the car toys, they are soaked.

"My tail is very wet, Fishhooks!" says Cuthbert.

"Squeezums, my fur is soaked," Dartmouth replies.

The Secret Cap is only magical when it flies the toys out of the car. So they leap into the garden.

"Squeezums! What a good job we got out." They paddle around the drive. "Fizz is made of carbon dioxide gas, then mixed with water and forced into bottles and cans at very high pressure, Squeezums. It is tingling froth which makes us burp!" Cuthbert is impressed with Dartmouth's knowledge.

"I have a joke for you, Fishhooks. What do you call a donkey with only three legs?"

"Humph," says Dartmouth. "A wonkey! Ha-ha." The Secret Cap whistles.

"Squeezums, back we go," says Dartmouth. As they settle down, both rather wet still in the car, Cuthbert's tail catches the radio volume control.

When Mum switches the engine on, an enormous sound blares out, *boom. Boom. Boom.* The twins cover their ears, Mum quickly switches off the volume control.

She then notices some puddles on the well of the car. "Why is it all wet here? Which of you two left a loose lid on the fizz, and who turned up the radio?"

As usual, Oliver and Lewis answer together, "Not us, Mum." We know what happened, don't we?

Chapter 7

Minehead

"Where is the sea?" called Oliver and Lewis together.

"The tide is out, we'll have to make sandcastles." They load up the beach things climbing over the grassy edge to the sand.

Suddenly, they hear a piercing siren then an orange and blue boat comes whizzing across in the distance. "That's the lifeboat, I expect it's going to rescue someone," Oliver says.

Gradually, the tide comes in. The twins wait anxiously to see whose sandcastle lasts the longest before the sea washes them away.

Meantime what are the car toys up to? Mischief no doubt. Having rubbed the Secret Cap *chuff, chuff, chuff* they find themselves on the footplate of the local steam train which is waiting on the line at the station, near the car park, for the next passengers. "Steam trains need lots of coal in their fire pit to make the steam that drives the very big train along the track," says Dartmouth.

"Come on, Squeezums, let's load some coal," he calls. The train driver and the fireman are away having their tea break. Soon Cuthbert is black from head to toe, using the shovel.

 Dartmouth pulls the hooter cord. *Toot, toot, toot, toot.* Passengers are surprised and rush to get on board. The family get on too. "Quick, rub the Secret Cap Cuthbert," calls Dartmouth, "they mustn't see us."

They just manage to scramble back to the car as the family chuff along the line on the train for 20 miles, there and back. "My joke, Fishhooks, today will surprise you – what do you call a train that sneezes? Achoo-choo train."

"Humph," says Dartmouth.

"Why is Cuthbert black?" asks Mum as they drive for home later.

"I don't know," says Oliver peering over the front seat. We know, don't we.

Chapter 8

Auntie Jean's for Tea

The family leave the car. Cuthbert rubs the Secret Cap. They both fly into the garden.

"This is fun, Fishhooks," Cuthbert calls.

"It's OK, Squeezums," says Dartmouth looking around the lawn. "Here's a jungle, let's explore." They leap about in the very tall grasses that sway above their heads. "These are called Pampas Grasses and mainly come from South America. They look like feather dusters and have very tough stems," brainy Dartmouth remarks. "What is a monster's favourite game Fishhooks? Swallow the leader."

"Humph," says Dartmouth smiling slightly.

"Let's have a fight," Squeezums says pulling off a broken frond. Dartmouth has a job finding one to break off.

"Mind my ears, Squeezums!" They scamper about in and out of the jungle waving their long wands, sending feathery seeds flying everywhere.

When they hear Secret Cap's gentle whistle, they drop everything and fly back to their car seat.

What a mess they left on the lawn, not to mention the seeds all over the car seat and floor!

"We haven't had any wind to blow it everywhere?" says Auntie Jean when she comes out to see the family off. She is still scratching her head as the car leaves.

Mum says, "Did you do that Oliver and Lewis?"

"No, Mum," they answer in chorus.

We know what happened, don't we.

Chapter 9
Trampoline

"Lovely new thing in the garden," Fishhooks says peering over the window ledge in the car.

"OK, rub the Secret Cap and out we go, Squeezums!" he calls to Cuthbert.

"Oops I'm flying – my tail keeps smacking my nose."

"You go higher than me," grumbles Dartmouth, waving a hairy paw in the air. Guess what they have found in the boys' garden – a trampoline!

"Oh I'm dizzy, Squeezums."

"So am I, Fishhooks!" Before they can get the right way up again from all that bouncing *ding ding* the Secret Cap sounds. "Quick they're coming out!" The toys fly so fast back to the car, Cuthbert sits upside down and Dartmouth lands on his tail under the seat belt.

"Why are the car toys in a muddle?" says Mum as she tidies them up. We know, don't we.

Cuthbert whispers his joke as the twins are in the car, "Why was six scared of seven, Fishhooks? Because seven eight nine!"

"Humph," goes Dartmouth.

"What makes us bounce, Squeezums, is called gravity. The heavier we are, the higher we can bounce," explains Dartmouth.

"I expect the twins can bounce higher than us Fishhooks," remarks Cuthbert.

Oliver and Lewis, the twin boys that sit at the back of the car, are always arguing. Every day the toys find different things hit them over the seat. One time, Oliver posts Lewis' trainer over the headrest gap hitting Cuthbert on the nose;

another time Lewis posts Oliver's school book over there, it hides Dartmouth's eyes, so he can't see where they are going. The toys never know what is going to land on them next. Mum doesn't see as she is busy driving.

The car is not as calm looking as it seems, on the way to school, is it!

Chapter 10
Big Plastic Umbrella

"What have they left in the car now, Squeezums?" grumbles Dartmouth, wriggling about.

"Fishhooks let's go," calls Cuthbert tries to grab the long stick which Mum has left leaning on him. He rubs the Secret Cap.

They land in the park in a heap, the big plastic umbrella opens suddenly as Dartmouth catches the handle. The wind turns it upside down and the point sticks in the ground.

"Come on, Fishhooks, jump inside." Squeezums is rocking jerkily side to side. They both sit watching through the plastic cover as the doggies are running in the park. "Shhh, Fishhooks, they haven't seen us in here." Suddenly, a gust of wind pulls the brolly up into the air. Luckily, they are both holding the handle. It lands in a bush with the handle upwards.

"This is like a boat, let's get down to the pond," squeaks Cuthbert. They rock about and the umbrella floats down onto the pond, just missing two toy boats. "This way to shore Squeezums we must lean to one side." Dartmouth having been a sailor knows how to get out of the water. Secret Cap whistles.

"Rub it, Squeezums, hurry!" The umbrella won't close. It is left sitting near the car as the car toys fly together to their seat.

"What is brown and sticky, Fishhooks?" whispers Cuthbert who is always ready with a joke. "The answer is a stick." He laughs.

"Humph," says Dartmouth as usual. Hearing the surprised calls from Oliver and Lewis, they peep over the window ledge just in time to see the twins rescuing the umbrella. Mum folds it down and puts it back in the car. "It isn't raining, boys, why did you get the brolly out?" They shake their heads. We know what happened, don't we!

Part 3

Chapter 11

Builders' Yard

"Off we go to get Dad's cement for mending the drive." Mum calls to the boys. They all see big muddy builders' trucks, heaps of red bricks and an enormous crane with wheels that are as big as the car. Driving in to the visitors' car park, the family get out for a look around.

"Where are we, Squeezums?" calls Dartmouth, peering over the window edge.

"Come on out, this looks fun Fishhooks." Rubbing the magic Secret Cap the car toys are soon flying over the enormous machinery in the yard. They soon get very dusty whizzing around the diggers.

"I'm going to sit in this digger bucket, Squeezums!" calls Cuthbert.

"I want to try the crane, Squeezums." Dartmouth clambers up the steep steps.

"Cranes are for lifting heavy equipment at building sites," says Dartmouth. "They have wire chain hoists and enormous wheels. They go very high in the sky. There are some new  ones called hydraulic crawler cranes with the latest engine and winch system."

"You know such a lot Fishhooks. Brainy," comments Cuthbert.

"I only know jokes – why do giraffes have long necks, Fishhooks?" he calls. "To keep their noses away from their smelly feet!"

"Humph!" remarks Dartmouth.

All back in the car with the bag of cement loaded in the boot for Dad. No one notices how dusty the car toys are.

"In the holidays shall we go to see Dancing Diggers?" suggests Mum.

"Hurray what a good idea!" chorus Oliver and Lewis.

We know why the car toys are so dusty, don't we.

Chapter 12

Driving Diggers

"Bring the car toys," says Mum.

They find themselves very high up in a very muddy field, each sitting on a twin.

Dartmouth's tummy is squashed on Oliver's lap. Cuthbert's tail is bent on Lewis' lap. They are each sitting inside the cab of a big yellow digger facing a pond with plastic ducks floating about.

"Pick up a duck with your grab," calls the digger Guide to Oliver. Dartmouth is shocked. He is not used to being out of the car. He shuts his eyes. He hopes everything will stop.

Oliver succeeds in hooking his little duck in the pond. He climbs down from the cab holding tight to Dartmouth. Lewis is still trying to catch his duck.

Cuthbert is shocked too!

"Well done boys," calls Mum as the twins climb down from the machines clutching their car toys.

"We'll put them back in the car before we go on the bigger diggers – we'll need both hands then."

"Thank goodness, Squeezums, I didn't like that," grumbles Fishhooks. "I'll tell you about diggers, Squeezums," whispers Dartmouth as they sit back safely in

43

the car. "They are called JCBs as they were invented by Joseph C Bamford. His are yellow and can be enormous. They are used for moving great heaps of soil  and gravel and mud when building things. Like the ones we saw today. Other companies make them too. Here are some green ones."

Cuthbert grabs his Secret Cap thankfully. "Sit still and I'll tell you a joke, Fishhooks."

"I don't really like jokes, Squeezums," he says. The both feel a bit queasy after their unexpected outing.

"I'll tell you anyway. Where do you weigh a whale, Fishhooks?"

"I don't know, Squeezums."

"At a whale-way station."

When the family return to the car, both toys are fast asleep. We all know where they've been, don't we.

Chapter 13
School Toy Day

"Reception can bring in a toy," say the twins' school.

"That's easy, we've already got Dartmouth and Cuthbert, haven't we Mum," said Oliver and Lewis together, "we don't need the others."

Dartmouth is surprised to be taken indoors, brushed and have a white, pointy unicorn horn attached between his ears with elastic. Cuthbert just had his Secret Cap firmly tied under his chin. Next morning in the car they both feel funny. "What is happening Squeezums?" grumbles Dartmouth.

"Don't know Fishhooks," he calls using their secret names for each other.

They find themselves being lifted out and paraded around the school playground. Oliver carries Dartmouth and Lewis has Cuthbert.

"Your baby dragon is tiny," says Lewis's friend.

"He's not very old, he can't breathe fire and his wings haven't grown yet."

"He's a lovely green colour," says Maisie.

"That's a funny brown teddy bear; he doesn't look at all like a unicorn." Oliver's friends laughs.

"Well, he was a unicorn once, but he kept eating too much porridge so turned into a furry bear," explains Oliver.

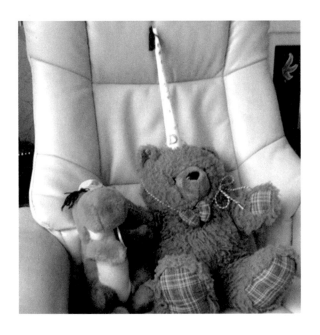

After the parade, Dartmouth and Cuthbert both win prizes for being VERY CUDDLY TOYS. Mum tucks them back in their place under the seat belt at the front of the car. They both sit feeling very proud wearing their winner's red rosettes. "My joke today Fishhooks is: what do elves learn at school? Don't know? The elf-a-bet!"

"We went to Reception Class today, Squeezums; this is the name of the first year of Primary School after Nursery School," said Dartmouth. "Oliver and Lewis are just aged five; they came in September. Do you remember when we went to nursery with them? They will now be learning lots of interesting things like adding up and writing about dinosaurs."

Mum drives home without the boys as they had a football game after school. She will fetch them at teatime. The car toys fall asleep after their busy day.

Chapter 14
Woolly Hats

"I can't see Squeezums," says grumpy Dartmouth. "That red woolly hat looks cheerful, perched over one ear, so smile Fishhooks," says his friend. The twins leave their woolly hats on the front seat as they go to the cinema. No need to rub the Secret Cap, the car toys could have fun. "Oh this green floppy one covers me all up Fishhooks," called Cuthbert in a muffled voice as they jump up and down outside their seat belt.

"You can get knitted, sewn, embroidered headgear of all styles," says Dartmouth. "The army says a third of your body heat goes out of your head." Dartmouth, as usual has lots of facts at his paw tips. "If you're bald, you can get sunburn, and if you have too much hair you can't see where you're going. So everyone has to wear a hat sometime."

"Let me out, Fishhooks. I'm lost in here." Cuthbert's little tail swished madly about, knocking the buttons on the dashboard of the car. "My new joke," he puffs , "is what did the hat say to the scarf, Fishhooks?"

"Humph," says Dartmouth.

"You hang around and I'll go on ahead!"

Luckily, the Secret Cap works so they manage to pull off their coverings before the family returns and they all take their seats.

"Why is the air conditioning working in mid-winter?" Mum asks the twins. "I don't think I switched it on." The boys didn't answer.

We know what happened, don't we.

Chapter 15

In the Woods

"Why are we sitting on all these leaves, Squeezums?" asks Dartmouth. "They're a bit prickly."

"Now the family have gone for a walk we can climb that log, Fishhooks." The car toys have been left on the picnic rug in the woods. Cuthbert jumps up and scrambles along a fallen tree trunk. "Look how high I am," he calls, waggling his tiny tail back and forth.

"These leaves have all fallen from the oak tree, they were green now they're turning brown as it's autumn, Squeezums. Oak leaves have wiggly sides and are quite big."

Dartmouth pads around in the crunchy leaves. He looks up through the branches. "I can see the sky." He points his paw upwards. He overbalances. "Whoops."

"You do look funny, Fishhooks, I can only see your ears sticking up." Cuthbert climbs even higher on his log. Dartmouth gets up and grumpily tries to brush the leaves from his fur. "I can't get down, Fishhooks, where's my Secret Cap to rub?" Dartmouth searches, peering down a rabbit hole.

"Not here, Squeezums."

"I'll jump onto you."

"Ow, ger off!" Cuthbert lands on Dartmouth's tummy. Suddenly they see the Secret Cap.

"Thank goodness. Back to the car quickly, Fishhooks, and I can tell you my new joke. What do you call a train that sneezes?"

"Humph, I don't know."

"A choo-choo train." Cuthbert sneezes.

"That's funny," says Mum when they get back to the car. "I am sure we left the car toys on the rug in the woods." The twins don't know what happened.

We do though, don't we.

Chapter 16

On the Pond

Mum drives the car to the park. Oliver and Lewis are going to play football with their friends. The car toys are looking for mischief as usual. They rub the Secret Cap and find themselves just next to the boating lake. Several model boats are waiting to have their motors started so they can race across the water. Dartmouth and Cuthbert discover a group of small sailing boats moored by the jetty. "Come on, Fishhooks, let's undo their ropes and see them sail away." Cuthbert runs along pulling the loops on each boat.

"Boats are called yachts when they have sails. Yachts only go the way the wind blows their sails, Squeezums, so to come back they have to zigzag across the wind, this is called tacking."

"You know so much, Fishhooks," says Cuthbert. They hide behind a nearby bush to watch all the boats sailing with the wind.

Suddenly all the owners are running along the shore. "My boat is sailing by itself," calls one girl.

"So is mine," says someone else. The twins walk by on their way back from football.

"Why are all the yachts in the middle of the lake, Mum?" The Park Keeper has to rescue their boats with his special hook.

He pulls them all in to shore. "Be more careful children," he says. "I don't know why they came loose. Perhaps the swans had something to do with it." The Secret Cap has flown the car toys back to the car.

"Fishhooks, what do cows do for fun?"

"Humph," says Dartmouth.

"They go to the moooovies."

Mum and the twins are as puzzled as the park keeper about the yachts, but we know what happened, don't we.

Chapter 17

In the Garage

"Stop kicking me, Fishhooks, we can't fly as I've dropped the Secret Cap on the floor," complains Cuthbert. Dartmouth winds down the window. "Let's jump," says Cuthbert.

"Gosh it's dark in here, Squeezums, where are we? What a lot of noise." *Bang, bang, bang.* As the car toys run away from the car, it rises up in the air on huge legs. They are in a garage where the car is being fixed. There is no sign of their family. "Let's hide in this big cupboard till the car comes down again," Dartmouth says. "I know they have to check the brakes, sump and exhaust and various cables underneath the car; that is why they put it up on the ramp," Dartmouth explains.

There are tools hanging everywhere. Cuthbert jumps on the weighing scales which *ping* and startle Dartmouth. Cuthbert opens a drawer and six boxes of screws fall all over the floor with a loud clatter. Dartmouth sits on a shelf next to lots of bottles. One tips over and spills down on top of Cuthbert.

Suddenly the door opens and a mechanic sees the two car toys. "Oh dear, I'm sorry Squeezums," whispers Dartmouth. With another loud bang the car is down again. Without the Secret Cap they have to wait for Mum, Oliver and Lewis to collect the car.

"I found your toys," says the mechanic. "The green one is rather oily so I wrapped him in newspaper."

"Thanks very much," says Mum carefully putting Cuthbert on the floor of the car. "You'll have to go in the washing machine. Dartmouth seems clean." Next day a newly sparkling Cuthbert is re-united with his friend Dartmouth as usual on the front passenger seat, under the seat belt.

"Thank goodness my warm breath is still working. I don't want it to get too hot, I am a dragon you see, Fishhooks. My joke I just thought of when I was whirling around in the tumble drier is: why did the tomato blush bright red? 'Cos it saw the salad dressing! Do you get it Fishhooks?"

"Humph." He grunted. He felt very happy to have his favourite baby dragon back beside him.

We know how Cuthbert got so dirty, don't we.

Chapter 18

A Grassy Field

Mum is loading the twins up with the picnic things after they park the car in the farmer's field.

It is a hot sunny day; there is an enormous noisy machine working in the next field. "What is that Fishhooks?" says Cuthbert as they peer out of the car window. "It is called a combine harvester, Squeezums. It has an engine and a conveyor belt to gather all the hay or straw in the field, bind it into round bundles with twine and wrap each one in black plastic sheeting. Each bundle is pushed out of the back as the harvester goes along."

"They look like black monsters, Fishhooks."

"Later a tractor and trailer will load them all up to store at the farm for the winter," continues Dartmouth.

Rubbing the Secret Cap the car toys fly out of the car, landing with a bump on top of one of the monsters.

The combine stops and the farmer goes off for lunch. "Let's explore," Cuthbert calls jumping down.

Dartmouth manages to slide down the side before they climb the steep steps into the combine cab. "Don't touch anything, Squeezums," says Dartmouth. Too late – Cuthbert swings on a lever and the whole bucket lifts into the air throwing lots of loose straw everywhere.

"Oh I like this Hamster Fishhooks."

"No, now look what you've done – rub the Secret Cap quickly."

Back in their seat. "I love that hamster, Fishhooks, I wonder what else I could make it do?"

"It's called a combine harvester, Squeezums, not a hamster." They sit in the car covered in straw.

"My joke today is: what do cats like to eat, Fishhooks? Can you guess? Mice cream."

"Humph," says Dartmouth.

Mum and the twins arrive to put everything back in the boot after a lovely day. Oliver and Lewis climb into the back as usual. "Why is there straw all over the front seat?" asks Mum.

The twins don't know, but we do, don't we!

Chapter 19

Going to the Garden Centre

"I can see lots of flowers, Fishhooks," Cuthbert calls as the family leave the parked car at the Garden Centre. "Let's explore." He rubs the Secret Cap and they fly to the water features.

"That's a fountain, Squeezums," remarks Dartmouth. Cuthbert jumps up and puts both feet and his little tail in the top bowl of three in the waterfall. "Whee – look at me Fishhooks." Dartmouth is carefully walking along a wet gravel stream with stone bears along the edge.

"They look like me, but they haven't any fur," he notices. He pats a large statue which falls over in the stream, blocking it. Soon there is a flood of water spreading over all the other ornaments. Cuthbert immediately jumps into the enormous puddle that is spreading onto the shop floor. "Water always finds the lowest place," says Dartmouth splashing along the path, not noticing how wet he is getting. "Water has no colour or taste or smell. It is very good for us to drink. Rain is saved in big lakes called reservoirs," he continues. "Then it is piped underground and comes out in our taps."

Cuthbert is already investigating a bright red cupboard which has a big picture of ice cream on it. "Come in here

Fishhooks. I love ice cream." He goes inside this kiosk and finds a long handle sticking out. "Come and help me." Dartmouth puts one wet paw on it and they both tug. A mountain of fluffy ice cream pours out on the floor to join the puddle of water. Soon they are both covered in it. Luckily, the Secret Cap calls at that moment and they fly back to the car. They lick each other clean. "My joke Fishhooks is what do you get if you pour hot water down a rabbit hole – hot cross bunnies!"

"Humph," says Dartmouth.

When Mum, Oliver and Lewis return and load the new plants they have bought in the boot, Mum says to the twins, "I wonder why they had such a flood in the Garden Centre today and asked us all to leave while they cleared it up?"

We know what happened, don't we!

Chapter 20
Easter Egg Hunt

Mum has hidden 20 small Easter eggs around the twins' garden. Five friends are invited to bring their favourite toy to hide under an umbrella each in case it rains. On Easter Sunday morning Dartmouth and Cuthbert are suddenly brought into the garden. Dartmouth finds himself plonked under some cabbage leaves in the vegetable garden. "Humph," he says to himself. "I wonder where Squeezums is." They have never been separated before.

Cuthbert is hidden under some very wet leek leaves. His tail waves anxiously as he searches for Dartmouth.

"Look for four eggs each and your toy – ready, steady, go!" calls Mum. Next to Dartmouth is Monty Monkey, he has hardly any fur as he is so old.

"Humph, can I share your umbrella, the cabbage leaves are dripping." Monty is shivering. "I hope they find us quickly," he says as he snuggles up to Dartmouth under a very bright stripey umbrella. Cuthbert sneezes as a leek leaf tickles his nose.

"Oh dear, I left my Secret Cap in the car."

Dartmouth and Monty Monkey are soon discovered. Oliver takes Dartmouth in the house and Maisie hugs Monty Monkey. "Well done, you've found them all," says Mum.

"I can't find Cuthbert," Lewis calls. Everyone is indoors as it has started raining. Poor Cuthbert is still sitting in the leek tops and is very wet. His tiny dragon breath is not hot enough yet to warm him. All the others are tucking into sausage and chips. Dartmouth is put on the hall seat ready to go back in the car later.

"I feel funny without Squeezums," he whispers to himself.

Mum and Lewis go down to the veg patch.

"Oliver hid him, I don't know where," says Lewis in a small voice. It is beginning to get dark as it is still winter.

Oliver is hiding under the sideboard secretly smiling to himself; he and Lewis are always teasing each other as they are the same age.

"Here he is under the leeks – he's so wet and dirty," says Lewis.

After he is cleaned up, Cuthbert is pleased to be warm and dry and the back in the car seat with Dartmouth. "I'll try not to leave my Secret Cap behind ever again, Fishhooks. I have got a joke though – What is a dinosaur called when he's sleeping? A Dino-snore!"

"Humph. I'll tell you about cabbages, Squeezums. The green ones grow to enormous sizes; children don't like them cooked, but they love coleslaw which is raw cabbage cut up and mixed with mayo and things."

"Yum," says Cuthbert.

We all know what happened today, don't we.

Chapter 21

The Shoe Shop

"Off we go to get your new shoes," says Mum. The twins complain. "You can take Dartmouth and Cuthbert with you, then afterwards we can go for burgers." Dartmouth and Cuthbert are surprised to be taken out of the car; Oliver has Dartmouth and Lewis has Cuthbert under their arms. The twins' feet are different sizes and have to have them measured with a special ruler. It takes ages. Jane the assistant pulls down lots of shoe boxes. The car toys are forgotten sitting under the bench.

"Let's go, Fishhooks." Cuthbert rubs the Secret Cap, they fly up high to the top shoe shelf.

"Great big boots," says Dartmouth putting his furry head right inside one. Cuthbert finds a large basket of shoe laces which all fall on the floor as his wiggly tail catches them. Then he jumps inside the boot box opened by Dartmouth. The lid shuts leaving him hidden inside. Dartmouth can't open it as his paws are too clumsy. Where is the Secret Cap? He sits scratching his head and looking down at the family below. The twins are holding their new shoe boxes.

"Let's go to the cafe now," says Mum. "Where are the car toys?" Jane the assistant is busy tidying up all the unwanted shoe boxes. A big search takes place.

Maisie and Monty Monkey come in and wonder what all the fuss is. "There he is," says Maisie looking up high on the top shelf. "Where's Cuthbert?" Cuthbert is very upset in the dark of the big boot box. His tiny dragon tail waves about frantically. He can't rub the Secret Cap as he is too squashed.

Bang, bang comes from the top shelf. Jane moves the sliding ladder along and climbs up. "Here he is," she calls, opening the lid.

"How did they get up there, and why is there a pile of laces on the floor?" says Mum.

We know, don't we.

Back at the car: "Fishhooks, my joke. What do ghosts eat? Spooketti!"

"Humph."

"I like those furry boots, they are for trekking in the mountains and the snow. The have big rough soles to grip with."

"You do know a lot, Fishhooks." They fall fast asleep after their exciting morning.